PEREGRINE'S
TALE

KEALAN PATRICK BURKE

For Norman Partridge

1

1979

HIS NAME WAS PERRY GRIFFIN, but before he'd learned the proper way to pronounce it, he'd simply run it together into one word: Per-grin, which as the years went by mutated into *Peregrine* in the mouths of all who repeated it. Annoyed at first by what he considered a ridiculous title, it wasn't until he realized what the name meant that he stopped trying to dissuade people from using it. An awkward child, he found the image of the bird of prey that came to mind whenever someone addressed him, to be somewhat bolstering, and more than a little cool. The christening of this new name, then, officially took place on his eighth birthday, when his mother presented him with his cake. Amid the twisted turrets of icing was a picture of a falcon in flight, its body skewered by dripping birthday candles, talons bared as it prepared to snatch its meal. Written in white icing across the cake was: HAPPY BIRTHDAY PEREGRINE. From then on, only the teachers at his school would insist on using his birth name. Everyone else used Peregrine, which the boy discovered meant "traveler," and though his ambitions of seeing beyond the woods in which he lived had not yet graduated beyond a mild curiosity, it would not be long before he was forced to live up to his name.

2

PEREGRINE DIDN'T BELIEVE IN GHOSTS, but only because he had never seen one. He heard the stories, of course, and sometimes lay awake attributing the chorus of night-sounds below his window to the wanderings of the dead, but always in the morning he would feel silly. The dead stayed dead, he knew. His mother had told him so and she had no reason to lie. The topic was occasionally broached in their house, but seldom discussed in-depth because for Peregrine, thinking about ghosts forced him to think of death, and that was infinitely more terrifying than anything that he might hear rustling around in the dark. So far as he knew, there was no proof that ghosts existed anywhere outside the realm of the campfire, but the reality of death could not be denied. It was a shadow the sun would never chase away, and the awesome inevitability of it terrified the boy to the core of his being.

Despite his convictions, however, he awoke one gloomy overcast morning to find a ghost sitting in the kitchen.

At least he assumed she was a ghost, for she would not look at him, but continued to stare at a point somewhere east of the window overlooking the woods. When he spoke to her, she did not answer, and after a prolonged moment of indecision, Peregrine went to his mother's side and shook her. She was cold. Still, she did not move, or acknowledge his presence. She just stared, her rocking chair frozen in mid-swing by the heel of her tattered gray slipper. Frightened, the boy followed her gaze but saw nothing he deemed worthy of such intense focus.

He spoke; she ignored him.

He wept; she was silent.

A newspaper sat folded on the table, with only the word 'MURDER!' visible above a grainy photograph and lines of tiny print. On the stove, the pots and pans were cold, the customary smell of bacon and eggs absent from the air. There was only the smell of woodsmoke as the embers of last night's fire hissed and spat, as if to assure the curious that there was life in its ashen bones yet.

Beyond the window, low purplish clouds rolled over the woods, rumbling. A flock of Canadian geese honked their way across the bruised pallet of the sky, plowing forth through a strengthening wind as lightning made dark veins of the trees.

Peregrine swallowed, panic clawing its way up his throat. "Mom?"

She didn't answer. He was beginning to feel as if he'd woken up in a strange house, or a nightmare. He wished for the latter, because all nightmares had to end eventually.

His mother hadn't combed her hair—a lapse in her strict daily routine that only reinforced his unease. Her eyes were wide and bloodshot, as if she hadn't slept. A part of him he had to struggle to ignore wondered if she was dead, if she had seen him to bed last night then come downstairs to sit in her favorite chair and die. She had certainly been quiet and sad enough over the past few weeks, ever since The Man left. Maybe the sadness had stopped her heart?

The mere thought of such a thing almost stopped his own.

Gently, so as not to startle her if she was simply lost in a fanciful daydream, he put his slim fingers on the arm of her chair, pausing when the pressure made it creak forward a notch. He hoped the movement wouldn't hurt her heel, braced as it was against the runner. Breath held, he drew close enough to her to notice that only the faintest scent of perfume lingered on her skin. Another ritual missed. She always squirted some on her neck just before she made him breakfast. Eggs and bacon, usually. Sometimes waffles, if he had done something to make her proud.

But there were no waffles this morning, and he couldn't remember the last time he'd made his mother proud, couldn't remember the last time he'd seen her smile. Ever since The Man left, slamming the door and leaving only a waft of whiskey, cigarettes, and sweat in the air behind him, she hadn't been herself.

Peregrine had done everything he could think of to cheer her up, but nothing worked. As the days passed and The Man didn't return, her face grew so tight and pinched he gave up trying to make her smile for fear it would split like an overripe melon.

The chair creaked again, and his heart leapt. He leaned closer, listening for the reassuring sound of her breathing, then gently, gently, pressed his ear to her chest.

When he didn't hear the slightest sound, he almost screamed, but before the horror could claw its way out, a dull thud sounded and he lunged forward, forgetting his concern for his mother's foot in favor of confirming what he hoped and prayed he'd heard.

Thudump.

He smiled.

Thudump.

Allowed himself to breathe.

Thudump.

"Mom?" he whispered and drew back to peer into her wan face.

She was no longer watching the wall. Her eyes had found him. He was almost overwhelmed with relief. *She's alive.*

"Mom?"

Her eyes were still glassy, but at least she'd shown some sign that she could see him. She was not a ghost, after all.

"Mom?" he said again, wishing more than anything that she would answer, even if only to tell him to shut up. "Can you hear me?"

But to his disappointment, she frowned, just a little, and her gaze returned to the wall.

I should call a doctor, Peregrine realized. *She's sick. There's something wrong with her. Why won't she talk?*

Although she hadn't spoken much at all after The Man walked out, she had at least moved and said a word here and there to him. She had continued to make him breakfast every morning, even though he could tell she didn't want to.

Secretly, he was glad The Man was gone. He remembered waking in his bed one night with the realization that it had been weeks since he'd last heard voices coming through the wall from his mother's bedroom. No voices, no booming laughter, no crying, no tortured squeaking of the bed, or moans, or animal grunting. Just quiet. Peregrine liked that just fine. He wouldn't be so tired in the mornings anymore after being kept awake by those godawful sounds; he wouldn't have to lie awake at night staring at the shadows the moon cast through the trees, wondering what peculiar things his mother and The Man were doing in her room. Wondering if The Man was hurting her. He wouldn't have to wait in bed in the mornings until he heard the sound of The Man's car starting up.

No, he didn't miss The Man at *all*. He'd rarely set eyes on him, but the glimpses he'd caught had been enough—a bearish man who wore large overcoats that only served to make him seem even bigger; hair long, dark and unruly;

spade-shaped face with coal-dark eyes glaring out above a bulbous nose and worm-like lips.

But mostly it was the smell of him that bothered the boy. Whenever The Man showed up, the house filled with a sickly-sweet smell so pungent Peregrine had to sleep with his face buried in the pillow. Even after the man was gone, the smell would linger for days afterward, as if there were dead flowers somewhere inside the walls.

Peregrine had learned not to ask about his mother's "guest" after his one and only inquiry had inspired her to knock out his two front teeth and chip a third with the edge of a frying pan.

His father was gone, and now The Man was gone too. He only had the faintest recollection of what his father had been like, but he missed him, if only because he had to have been better, and kinder, than the monster his mother had let into their house.

He tried to feel sorry for her, but it was difficult. He hated what the monster's absence was doing to his mother but was overjoyed and relieved that The Man was gone. Whenever that dead flower smell choked the house, it frightened him. The Man's oily shadow, slithering across the stair steps as if coming to get him, frightened him even more. He didn't care if he never saw him again.

Then an awful thought occurred to him: What if the only way he would ever get his mother back to herself was if The Man came back? What if the doctor called round, shook his head, clucked his tongue and suggested the only remedy was to fetch The Man at once. Then her mother's visitor might never leave, and that was too awful a possibility to contemplate. He could almost smell that terrible stench already, eager to be let back inside.

A bubbling whine in his stomach reminded him he had yet to eat, and after a final, longing look at his mother, he sighed and went to fix himself some toast. He released the arm of the chair and it heaved forward with an odd clattering sound. He looked in time to see an empty whiskey bottle spinning away from his mother's feet and watched as it came to rest pointing toward the window, like the needle of a compass following the direction of his mother's gaze.

Peregrine frowned and went to fetch the bottle. He couldn't remember ever seeing his mother drink liquor before. Perhaps The Man had left it behind.

As he slipped his hand around the bottle, there was another noise. Behind him. A scraping sound he couldn't immediately identify. He straightened, bottle in hand and turned.

A creak.

He jolted and almost dropped the bottle, then felt the tension drain from his body. A smile warmed his face. The rocking chair creaked again, settling back on its runners. His mother was awake, *proper* awake, and standing up, if a little unsteadily. It bothered him that she was still staring at the wall, though. He tried again to locate the object of her fascination but saw nothing but flaking paint and their cheap old clock, keeping time with his heart.

"Mom…you scared me," he said, reaching out a hand in case she needed to steady herself. Her lips parted with a dry rasping sound. She continued to sway, as if she was still in synch with the movement of the rocking chair. Peregrine moved closer. He wasn't sure he could do anything if she did fall over, but it was only right to try.

And then she did speak, though it took Peregrine a moment to decipher what she'd said.

Her voice was faint, little more than a whisper, so much so that at first, he thought it was the wind he'd heard fluttering through the gutters. But her mouth had moved to shape the words and there could be no mistaking they were hers.

She said: "He didn't want you."

Her eyes widened, as if she'd just realized something. Peregrine didn't think it possible for her skin to get any whiter than it was already, but it did. She was now so pale her eyes were like splotches of dark ink on a white sheet of paper.

Peregrine was confused. He'd seen drunk people before—in all the times they'd visited Uncle Marty in Indiana, he'd never once seen the old man sober—and wanted to believe his mother had simply had too much to drink, and that was why she was acting so weird, and saying things that made no sense.

But though young, he was no fool. He knew what her words *might* mean, but tried hard not to think about it.

She turned her head, just a fraction of an inch, and her eyes moved. Any joy or relief Peregrine might have felt at this was immediately obliterated by the cold fury he saw in them. Her hatred radiated out toward him, an almost palpable thing, hazing the air between them. She sucked in a deep, shuddering breath, and it emerged in a soft groan.

"Mom…what is it?"

"He didn't want you," she repeated, this time louder.

"Who?"

"'Him or me,' he said, and guess…who I chose?"

Peregrine was about to ask her to stop, tell her that she was frightening him, but an icy needle of realization slid into his brain and stole the breath from his lungs.

His mother blamed him for making The Man go away. He didn't think that fair at all, but knew it meant he'd be black and blue by bedtime. All because of that foul-smelling giant with the crawling shadow.

He made her choose between us. He was grimly satisfied that his hatred of The Man had been justified, but the fear overruled it. There was something in his mother's eyes he'd never seen before, and it made him want to run from her. But before he could move, his mother's left hand rose. He was now able to see what the scraping sound had been, and it made every hair on his body stand to attention.

It was the long cast iron poker that had always hung on its hook by the fireplace. His mother's knuckles were white around its faux bronze handle. She held it as if it were a sword, the business end whitened by ash and wavering in the air between them.

"'Children are like houses' he told me, 'You can always leave 'em and get yourself a new one if the old one starts to stink'." Tears spilled down her cheeks. Peregrine wished he could believe they were for him. "He wanted me to send you away so we could be together, so I could be happy. And don't you think that's only fair? Your father left me here alone, with nothing but bills and no money, no fucking *life!* How is that fair, huh? That I have to spend my whole life cooped up in here with you while the rest of the world gets to live their dreams and ambitions. Tell me, Peregrine…how is that *fair?*"

Peregrine shook his head, wishing now that she'd stayed in her trance. He knew protesting and pleading was useless. When she lost her temper she would talk and beat him at the same time, her efforts increasing if he tried to wriggle away or apologize for whatever had incited her fury. This was no ordinary temper though. He had never seen such alien hatred in his mother's eyes, and it terrified him. Helpless, he stood frozen, legs trembling, while above the house the sky bellowed, and white light seared the windows.

She was steady for a moment, momentarily distracted by the burgeoning storm, then her gaze flitted back to Peregrine, and she smiled.

It was the most hideous thing he'd ever seen. He had done nothing wrong and yet in a heartbeat his mother had become a monster, just like The Man. He wanted to know where his mother had gone, the mother who'd joked with him over breakfast for years, hugged him and protected him…and loved him. He wondered if that's what The Man had been doing to his mother at night—poisoning her somehow. For there was no love in the eyes of the woman towering over him now.

"Mom…" he whispered.

"But I turned him down," she said, still smiling that terrible smile, "I let another man walk out of my life with my dreams in his pocket."

"Please…"

"But you know something, Peregrine. *You're* not going to leave with anything of mine. Nothing."

It seemed the air grew heavy then, as she took an uneven step forward, the weight of the poker conspiring with gravity to drag her to the floor. Peregrine felt a cold streak of despair freeze the flesh between his shoulder blades and he began to sob.

It was a mistake.

"Don't you cry, Peregrine," his mother said and in the next flash of lightning, her smile was gone, pulled back into an inhuman snarl that heralded her killing blow. "Don't you fucking dare cry!" She steadied herself and raised the weapon over her head.

"Please Mommy…"

For a split second, Peregrine thought he saw a flicker of doubt cross his mother's face, but then it was gone and he knew by the way her body tensed that she was preparing to hit him. He braced himself for unimaginable pain, perhaps the last he would ever feel.

There was a whoosh as the poker came down and Peregrine wailed, hands raised to ward off the blow. Thunder rolled boulders across the roof. The wind buffeted the house. Instinct forced him to dodge the arc of her strike and he staggered back a few steps, hands still in front of him as if will alone could make a metal shield of his fingers.

"Don't…"

She shrieked and drew her arm back, eyes so wide he could only see the whites and in that moment, he realized his mother was truly gone. The lightning made a witch of her, a foul, snarling thing straight out of a Grimm Fairy Tale.

"Trust me, Peregrine. It will be better for us both when you're gone."

She swung the poker at his head but this time he didn't wait for it. Despite the terror that made his limbs feel full of lead, he broke for the door, phantom pain already punching icy holes in his skull. But all he felt was the poker cut the air; all he heard was his mother's enraged cry; and then he was colliding painfully with the kitchen table, spinning, then once more running, the short path to the front door reeling away from him as it might in dreams and nightmares.

The poker whooshed again and connected with something that shattered on impact. Peregrine did not stop or look back to see what had taken the blow meant for him. He fumbled at the door handle with panicked fingers. It wouldn't open. Behind him, his mother's breath whistled through her nose and the sound drew closer.

He wrenched at the door handle once, twice, and again but it wouldn't budge. He pounded desperately at the wood. Weeping uncontrollably, snot dribbling from his nose, he shook his head, denying the cruel reality he had suddenly found himself thrust into, and punched the door hard enough to crack his knuckles. The pain brought a new wave of sobs and he almost gave up, almost sagged to the floor to await a punishment he didn't deserve.

"Wait there, Peregrine," his mother commanded, her breathing like a bellows in the small room. "I'm going to fix it."

She was behind him, he heard her thump against the kitchen table, only a few feet away.

"Wait for me. I'll make it better. John will come back. You'll see."

John. The Man. The Devil.

"You'll see," she said again, and now she was towering over him.

"Please," he whimpered and almost felt the air strain as she hefted the poker again.

"Hush now," she soothed.

She locks the door, he realized then and his chest almost exploded with hope. Every night she locks the door. In his panic, he had forgotten.

He lunged forward.

The poker whipped through the air.

He fumbled, grabbed, snapped back the lock and pulled.

The door opened, but not before the wicked iron thudded against his back, almost crippling him. He screamed. Fireworks erupted before his eyes and liquid flame raced up his spine. For a fleeting instant, he wondered if she'd killed him, if the floating, dizzying sensation meant he was now a ghost. He staggered, collided with the door, forcing it to close. The darkening light of morning recoiled from the jamb.

Peregrine choked on his own cries, then forced himself to stand. The muscles in his back sang with agony. Needles danced across the skin. It felt as if a cannonball had been shot into him, but despite the torture of standing, he managed it. Knew he had to. He was not yet dead. There was still a chance to get away.

"You're making this harder than it needs to be…"

Her words were muffled, as if his ears had been stuffed with cotton.

His hands, trembling so badly he missed the doorknob twice and ended up scrabbling at the lock, finally found purchase and he tugged with all the strength he had left.

Daylight, tainted by the storm, seeped in again and this time he lurched forward, blindly, hands outstretched to grab freedom, even as stars peppered his vision. The pain raged, tried to drag him to the ground.

Outraged screams trailed him as he blundered out into the rain. The sky boiled black and silver, the clouds churning. Thunder crackled and split the heavens.

Peregrine stumbled on.

3

H E STUMBLED ACROSS THE YARD, collided with the fender of his mother's Buick, then quickly made for the woods that stood patiently on the borders of the property. Thick limbs of spruce tried to slow his passage, but he fought through them until the air around him grew denser and the light faded. When he paused and took in his surroundings, he could see nothing but trees, some dead and fallen, most standing tall and creaking in the wind.

A fresh wave of fear flooded through him. He had been in the woods a thousand times, but never when the light was seeping from the day. Never when a storm was shredding the sky over the trees, and never to escape death at the hands of his own mother. He bent a hand back to knead the throbbing at the base of his spine, recalling as he did so when he'd asked his mother why Uncle Marty walked around with one arm permanently crooked behind his back.

Spine trouble, she'd told him.

As he trudged his way through the trees, picking his way over deadwood and avoiding critter holes, he thought he finally understood the pain Uncle Marty had had to live with. He wondered if that was the reason the old man drank so much.

The sky thrust a spear of lightning and cracked the earth somewhere up ahead. The furor made Peregrine hunker down, his arms clasped protectively around his head. He was still crying, but the tears were near their end, his eyes swollen and sore. A startled bird fluttered from the brush and took to the air, quickly vanishing into the storm.

Why is she doing this to me? Peregrine thought, miserably. Already he wanted to go home. He liked the woods when it was light, but now that the light was almost gone, the place looked almost as hostile as his own home had become. In all likelihood there might be worse things waiting for him out here. It also occurred to him that if he wandered too far and it got dark, he might get lost and die out here anyway, so he continued on until he was far enough away from the house, but not so far that he couldn't find his way back if he needed to, found a rotted stump, and sat. His back protested by tugging the muscles tight, pain thrumming along his spine. He winced.

Thunder rumbled; the rain sizzled down around him.

How could she choose him over me?

Confusion buzzed within him as he stared at the carpet of twigs, pine needles, and moss beneath his feet. Cold droplets weighed down the leaves of a walnut tree close by and he watched them dripping.

It was The Man's fault, The Man who had turned his mother against him.

"John," he said aloud, as if it were a curse word.

He imagined *John* now, stalking around the corner of the house. His mother would drop the poker and run to him, joy on her face, her arms wide to receive her guest. She would shower him with affection and bring him inside out of the storm, maybe for some hot soup and some dry clothes. A warm bed. And when he asked what had happened with Peregrine, his mother would smile and shrug and tell him: *Spine trouble.*

An involuntary moan slid from Peregrine's mouth. His shivering intensified, but there was rage there now, shaking him from the inside out. *She doesn't want me. She doesn't care.*

Amid the fury, he tried desperately to latch onto a memory of better times, but his head was pounding, the shivering making his teeth click together. All the good times seemed forced and contrived now. Every kind word, every kiss on the cheek, every promise…all lies, all an act. His mother had been stringing him along…using him until her knight came along to take her away to better things. He snorted laughter then, and the sound of it was so alarming, he flinched and huddled in on himself.

No, you've got it wrong. She's just a little sick, that's all. She needs help.

Maybe that was true, but it didn't change the fact that she was trying to kill him. If he tried to tackle the twelve-mile walk into town, she'd only have to take the car and she'd have caught up to him in minutes. The only other option was to wait it out in the darkening woods with the storm forcing the trees to dance around him.

He didn't think it possible for the rain to get any heavier, but it did, and when it pelted his scalp hard enough to sting, he stood, sodden and trembling and screamed at the trees, at the house beyond, and at the evil, wicked woman who'd pretended to be his mother all these years:

"I don't care if you kill me! You don't love me anyway! You only love *him*."

Thunder responded and it made the forest seem full of ravenous creatures, their dark bellies roiling with hunger. Lightning splashed its cobalt shadow over the trees. Peregrine, fists clenched, teeth gritted, turned to his left and walked on, away from the house and deeper into the woods. He ignored the pain in his back, though now it seemed as if the last flash of lightning had set it aflame. Nevertheless, thoughts of escape helped him maintain the pace. He was still afraid, still weeping. He felt betrayed and unsure. He wanted to go home, to open the door and find his mother sitting by the fire, mad only with worry, and looking just like she had in the old days. Before *John* came. Peregrine would tell her he'd gotten lost in the woods and fallen asleep, and she would scold him, but with love in her eyes. She would cry, her skin soft, her perfume untainted by alcohol as she drew him into her embrace. Then she would carry him upstairs to sit with him until the storm moved on. The thought almost stopped him in his tracks. The hope was so strong he wondered if, as in some of the stories he'd read, a wish could really come true if you wanted it badly enough.

Heartsick, he moved on. Real life was nothing like that. In real life, mothers pretended to love their children and beat them for no reason. Sometimes, they even tried to kill them.

"Peregrine."

He stopped dead. Every muscle grew taut.

Imagination, he told himself. *I imagined it. There's no one here but me.*

Overhead, the trees swished like ocean waves in the wind, while those with bare branches tapped gnarled knuckles together. The sky sounded as if it would come tumbling down around him.

He turned.

"Mom?"

She was standing behind him.

His most recent imaginings made him relieved to see her, even though wet and shivering, she looked more like a witch now than ever before. Her hair hung in her face, the lightning revealing only a bone-white curve of cheek. She twitched, rain sluicing down her arms, her nightdress drenched so that he could see the bare flesh beneath.

He wanted to throw his arms around her, despite how she had hurt him, despite the certainty that she didn't love him and never had. Despite her betrayal. But he couldn't see her eyes through the sodden mop of her hair, and was sure if he could, they'd be filled with lightning. *She's gone*, he knew, and felt the last vestiges of hope flee on the wind.

At last, he convinced himself to turn and run, to keep going on until he reached town, and safety, but when he turned, her bony white hand clamped down like a steel claw—a *falcon's* claw—on his shoulder. He spun back to face her, intending to thrash and kick and bite his way free. And stopped.

She was holding the poker above her head. He'd waited too long. Now, she drew her hand back further still and muttered something the storm made difficult to hear. He wanted to believe it was *I love you*. But it sounded more like *Hush Now*.

His heart and soul ran and cleared the forest screaming, but his body stood and wept. Any minute now he would wake up, he knew he would.

The air crackled and for a moment seemed to shimmer, as if made of water. He watched it, weeping, as the storm exploded through the woods.

The poker came down.

Then all fell quiet in Peregrine's world as he died at his mother's feet.

4

PEREGRINE OPENED HIS EYES and fire filled them, sudden agony chasing away the words he dreamt had been whispered in his ear. And over the pain that shrieked at him now, he thought that maybe there had been a boy in his dream, a child his own age, who had been afraid of something. His fear had been palpable. Peregrine tried to recall more but a solid bar of pain clamped down between his eyes and he whimpered, rolled onto his side and was numbly aware of cold water seeping through his shirt. The rest of his dream floated away like a kite in the wind, still tethered but too far away to reach. For now, the relentless agony held court and he brought his hands to his temples and squeezed. A gentle breeze tousled his hair as he tried to raise his head. His brain ignited; he winced and coughed dark shadows onto the mossy carpet beneath him while his bones tried to initiate a dance the chaperone of pain denied.

Then, abruptly, there was a voice, and it dragged him out of his disorientation.

"She's gone."

With great effort, Peregrine turned his head. The first thing he noticed was the sunlight, which fell in lazy honey-colored streams and seemed not at all normal. The air itself was thicker, darker than it should have been and appeared to move with a subtle fluid-like grace. Now and again, something would ripple through it, like fish moving beneath the water, and it would distort the world around it. But however unusual these things were to the boy's pained eyes, when he tilted his head and looked up at the canopy of trees above him, he saw that up there, it was much worse.

The pines had been stripped of leaves, their trunks aged, and now they craned forward to regard him, their boles warped and twisted, infested with shadows which ran like oil from the bark. Branches wound downward with spindly fingers, each one resembling a hand that had been charred and broken. Every one of them seemed to be struggling to reach him. Thick slimy roots had been frozen while flailing from gaping maws in the floor of the woods, the leaves around them black.

Still dreaming, Peregrine thought. It had to be a fantasy, a nightmare from which he would soon awake. But would he feel this much pain in a dream?

Across from where he lay, a man sat on a felled tree, watching him.

"Who are you?"

"Who do you think?"

And now Peregrine knew it was a dream, because only a miracle could have brought his father back to him.

His father, who seemed to have been crudely whittled from ember and swollen dark and smelled of tobacco and turned earth. His father, a crooked question mark pressed against the deadfall.

His father, who had died, but only for a little while.

"Get up."

The boy rose, but only in his mind. A whirlwind of pain kept his body nailed to the floor. "I can't," he sobbed and was sure his tears were red. "It hurts." He became aware that one of his hands was soaked in blood. "It hurts," he repeated, and even his tears burned. His father clucked his tongue with the sound of a twig snapping.

"Get up. We've got work to do."

"I think I'm dying, Dad," he whimpered, as the pain exploded across his skull. "I think she killed me."

"Stop whining and get to your feet." The words were flat, the tone murderous, and now the boy could feel his father's cold hard eyes drilling through the back of his neck. "We're gonna set this right."

"I can't."

"I said, get *up*."

"Help me."

"I aim to help us both, but the getting up you have to do on your own."

It felt as if lead weights had been tied to his face, dragging it back down to a promise of painless sleep. He thought his brain might have been mashed to bits but was afraid to raise a hand—even if he could—to probe the damage there. Angry hornets stung his skull, but every attempt to shake away their assault threatened to send him spinning into oblivion. Besides, his father was here, and he dare not disappoint him, not when he'd gone to the trouble of raising himself from the dead to come get him, not when he was all Peregrine had left. He grit his teeth, held a breath that tasted like copper-colored vomit, and planted his hands on either side of him, palms sinking into the moss.

"That's it…"

He grunted and tried to push the carpet away into the

gloom that lay beneath him. Twigs snapped and pine needles stabbed his skin, but he ignored them. The fire turned to molten lava in his head, lapping against the backs of his eyes, sending hot rivers running from his nose, and in that moment, as he rose unsteadily, the breath escaping between the gaps in his teeth in a series of tortured hisses, he knew without a doubt that he was not dead. There could never be this much pain after death, unless you ended up in Hell, and he was pretty sure he hadn't done anything wicked enough in his eleven years of life to deserve that.

The air moved sluggishly around him. *Where am I?*

As if of their own volition, Peregrine's elbows continued to straighten, levering him up ever so slowly. The agony was unbearable, his body shuddering with the strain as his heart drove fiery blood into his head. Sweat ran in rivulets down his face. His eyes stung.

"Dad…" he whispered, pleading.

"Keep going." There could be no denying the voice came from his father, but the iciness was an alien thing. It frightened him, led him to wonder what the grave might have done to the man he'd loved.

"Why won't you help me?"

"It's not my place. Now do it, damn you."

The boy closed his eyes and pushed, pushed, pushed, imagining the world had tilted and made the forest floor an immense chamber door he needed to open if he wanted to escape the hurtful dark. His whole body vibrated as if electricity had been shot through his veins and he moaned. The struggle seemed to take hours, every moment marked by his father's tangible impatience, but at last he was able to draw his knees under him, relieving some of the strain from his trembling arms.

"Good boy."

He sat up and the world spun as fresh searing agony battered his skull. He winced, wept anew, and brought his hands up to find the wound. His hair was stuck to his scalp, hardened by old blood. Sobbing uncontrollably, he turned to look at his father.

"Why'd she kill me?"

"She didn't," his father told him. "But not for the want of trying."

"It was *him*, wasn't it? John."

"Yes, it was. You were an inconvenience."

"Did she…?"

"Enough questions. Time to find your feet."

He did, though it took even longer to stand than it had

to get on his knees, and it left him staggering, with nausea swirling through him. He was cold, and quaking, and sweating profusely. More than anything he wanted to sleep, in his own bed—the only place he could think of that might end this dreadful nightmare and see him safely back to the sunshine world: a place where a mother's love was pure, and violence was something that happened to everyone *else*.

"Good. Now we can go."

"Go where?"

His father rose. "To find your mother."

The boy frowned, his legs like jelly, and the words came out before he thought to stop them. "You're dead."

"Yes."

"How can I see you?"

"Because you've been made to."

Peregrine didn't understand but resisted saying so in case it made his father angry. Instead he asked, "What are we going to do when we find her?"

His father stood motionless for a moment. Then he turned and began to walk away. "We're going to set things right," he called back over his shoulder. "Teach them that people aren't houses. We're going to kill them."

The words were so wrong, so blasphemous, and so

terrible that Peregrine knew he should have felt terror seizing his heart, panic playing his nerves like violin strings. But he didn't. He felt a disorientating sense of *right*, that whatever happened once he started on this path would be as it was supposed to be. And while it scared him, he also realized he had no choice. He could not stay here, or risk going back to the house alone.

Father was here. Father would guide him.

On unstable legs, he took a few tentative steps. Each one sent thunder into his brain and he narrowed his eyes, willing it away. Still disturbed by the cast of this new reality, he nevertheless forced himself to quicken his pace. But as he stepped wide to avoid the tentacles of a pine tree, he stopped dead, startled to see that there were other people in the woods, watching him. A legion of people, their pale faces drawn, shadows leaking from their eyes as if their heads were pillowcases stained with oil.

A chill rippled through him. "Who are they?"

His father glanced sidelong at him, and now, in the amber daylight, as an unnaturally slow wind tugged at the trees and the crowd in the woods looked on, he saw that a thick dark fissure bisected his father's face, forcing his eyes too far apart. The eyes themselves were swollen with blood.

"Dad?"

"You brought them here, Peregrine," his father said. "You led all of us here."

He walked off, through the trees, pausing once only to check that his son was following. Peregrine trailed him at a distance, no longer sure he could trust this ruined image of the man he'd once known, and as he approached the watchers, they glared at him, as if he'd done something to draw their ire. For the rest of the journey, he averted his gaze from them, and tried to will away the pain that pulsed behind his eyes.

He had awakened into a place he didn't recognize, a place better suited to the fairytales—a haunted forest. And who knew what else might be hiding in the coiling dark? But no matter how frightening it was, it still didn't feel wrong, and as silent tears rolled down his face, he wondered what he would say when they found his mother; what *she* would say when she saw who had brought him to her.

Worse, he couldn't stop imagining how it was going to feel to watch her die.

5

H ERE THE NEW WORLD ENDED.

Peregrine stood at the entrance to the woods, the house standing a few feet away looking quiet and unassuming, as if a madwoman hadn't betrayed and attempted to murder her child here a few hours before.

But the boy was not looking at the house. He stood with his back to it, despite the fear that his mother might come shrieking out of it, poker raised, to finish what she'd started. The fear could wait. For now, awe had possessed him, as he watched the trees shift and bend and tremble in their dark amber world, a world he had stepped out of as simply as stepping over a crack in the pavement. It had tried to hold onto him, the thick air rushing into his lungs, the lazy amorphous light scrabbling at his back, but then he was free and gasping for breath while his father looked on. Now that world stood before him, framed by the trees, and it would only take a step to be immersed in its darkness once more. It was incredible. He had ventured into these woods hundreds of times, to play, or read, or play Robin Hood, and not once had he sensed anything amiss about it. The trees were just trees, the air sweet and clear. How could he have known that it was a fragile picture, pasted over something terrible? How could he ever have believed there was another world, another plane, waiting for him to see it?

"Peregrine."

He turned to face his father, who nodded pointedly at the house. "She's inside."

The boy looked at the house. He had been born and raised here. The cedar walls glistened from the recent rain. The lace curtains gave the windows a tired look. As he watched, a squirrel ran across the roof, walnut in mouth, and vanished behind the house. To anyone else, it would look like a quiet, peaceful place, as it had been for many years. But now it was a place of corruption, a poisoned, evil thing that had spat him out as soon as it was done with him. As soon as *she* was done with him.

"She's sleeping," his father said.

"What do I do?"

He watched an unconvincing smile quarter his father's cloven mouth as he dropped to his haunches and retrieved something long and black from where it had been hidden among the leaves. He turned and held it out to Peregrine.

The poker.

"Bring her into our world," he said.

6

LET HIM RUN LET HIM GO *let him get away!* Debilitating pain brought Peregrine to his knees, hands clutched to the sides of his head as if they might keep it from shattering. His vision jolted and he shut his eyes. The images came without warning, a stuttering film pulled through his head almost too fast to see, but figures lingered and rose like ghosts in his mind.

The boy again, and a railroad. It was clearer this time than it had been in the dream. A blond-haired boy, about Peregrine's age, running...

Not yours to keep we need him let him go...

There was a dead man chasing him.

And the whisper—

Don't touch him he's ours leave him alone...

It's my *voice,* Peregrine realized, his confusion deepening. *I'm telling him to leave the boy alone. But who is he?*

A moment later, there was nothing but darkness and the muttered jumble of his own thoughts. Gradually, the pain began to ebb away, until only the discomfort from his head wound remained. He opened his eyes, felt the weight of the poker in his clammy hand.

"Do it." His father stood close by, head bowed as if in prayer. "You won't be killing her, so quit thinking that. You'll be releasing her, freeing her."

As angry as he was, Peregrine didn't think he could do it. The mere thought of it appalled him. And what if he went inside and she wasn't sleeping? What if his father was wrong and she was waiting behind the door with an ax in her hand? What if The Man—*John*—was there? Then it would all be over.

Listen to yourself, said a voice he wasn't sure was his own. *You're afraid of harming her but you're worried she might kill you first. Sounds to me like you already know what must be done.*

He gave a slight shake of his head. "Why?" he moaned aloud, and his father was suddenly right there, gruesomely bisected face shoved into Peregrine's own.

"Because she *murdered* me, you little prick, and whether you like it or not, executing murderers is your job now. Hers is only the first of many lives whose fate you'll have to decide, and you'll get to like it, because you'll have to." With a snarl, he grabbed Peregrine by the collar of his shirt and flung him toward the door. "Now get to work. We have more visits to make after this one."

Peregrine staggered to a halt and looked pleadingly at his father. At length, the sorrow left his face, replaced by a flush of anger, "You're not my father, are you? No more than she's my mother anymore."

His father smiled. "Get it done. You'll have all eternity to ask her to forgive you when she's by our side."

Will she really come back? Peregrine felt sick and wondered what would happen if he just tossed the poker away and ran. Somehow, he didn't think he'd get very far.

The breeze tossed leaves at the house and smacked them against the window. Clouds obscured the sun and shadows crawled through the woods. When Peregrine raised his face, the crowd of ghosts had formed a circle around the house. Around *him*. A gathering of tangible figures, a phantasmagoria of flesh and blood men, women, and children, all of them unified by the expressions of undiluted contempt they wore. Torn faces, broken bones, and ruptured skin—a display of shattered things. They seethed and their hate kept him from running; the threat in their eyes kept him from trying.

This is the right thing to do, he told himself. I know it is, I feel it, even if I don't want it to be.

"Do it, boy."

Peregrine made one final, feeble effort to wake from the nightmare, but when he opened his eyes and saw the wet leaves beneath his shoes and the open door before him, he glanced down at the poker, tightened his grip on the cold handle, and entered the house.

7

S HE WAS IN HER ROOM, SLEEPING, just as his father had said. Her mouth was open. She sucked in great big breaths that scratched at her throat and made her snoring sound like the last choking gasps of a dying woman. Her hands were across her chest, fingers twitching as her dreams took sharp turns. A graying spray of auburn hair all but occluded the pillow.

Peregrine stood by the bed, watching her. *I can't do this. She's my mother. I love her.* This was not the woman who had tried to kill him, not the woman who had blamed him for her misery. This was his mother as he knew her, albeit without the noxious stench of whiskey that shared her room. This was how he'd found her whenever the nightmares had propelled him from his bedroom and into hers, with a plea on his lips for protection from the demons still stalking him. And yet this was the worst nightmare he'd ever had, and it seemed there would be no waking from it. And here she was in her bed, but it wasn't the same, no matter how much he wanted it to be. The reality of what he was doing here came crashing down and a loud sob escaped him.

"I'm sorry," he whispered, his mother's form melting and shattering as tears filled his eyes. "I'm so sorry."

Something eclipsed the daylight, painting shadows on the walls. Fearful, Peregrine looked away from his mother to her window, with its floral drapes and painted frame, to the dreadful aspect of his father's mutilated face pressed against the glass.

"See her," he said, his eyes so black they looked like pools of oil. "See her for what she is." Then the darkness clambered from his eyes in an explosion of tendrils, penetrating the glass without shattering it and climbing the walls, spreading outward, consuming the light at a frightening speed. The room darkened quickly, as if the curtains had been hastily drawn. Peregrine began to back away, his pulse quickening, breath rapid as he raised the poker to ward off whatever might lunge at him from the sepia-toned gloom. And he was certain something would. His skin crawled as the sensation of a million watching eyes flooded over him. His father seemed to grow and stretch until he'd filled the window, still spinning out oily black threads that had all but devoured the light in the room. Abruptly the air turned cold, licking Peregrine's skin with icy tongues. Overhead, the light bulb shattered. The pieces took impossible time in falling.

Rasping, hitching breath drew his gaze downward. To the bed.

To his mother, or what she had once been before the shadows had mauled her, leaving behind an ancient, crumbling thing with deep lightless caverns for eyes. On the pillow, soiled with inky smudges, her hair writhed, struggling to be free of her diseased skull. Dead. She had to be. And yet she moved. Some hideous trickery made her twitch and shift beneath the off-white sheets, still visible despite the increasing weight of darkness. Amber light dappled the walls, *beneath* the walls, glowing dully from under the flaking paint. He should not have been able to see her, would have preferred blindness to looking at what she had become, but her bed it seemed was the sole source of illumination in the room, possessed of a purity that seemed alien in this awful room, and incongruous given the monstrosity atop it.

"Oh, how we laughed," she said, her lips moving slower than she spoke. "How we laughed about what I was going to do to you."

"Stop it," Peregrine said, but not to her, not to anyone but the unseen engineer of this horror. "I want to go home." On some level, he knew he was home, but fear compelled him to beg for a return to the sane safe place, the *other* place, where mothers didn't try to kill their sons and darkness was only an absence of light, not a cloak used by unspeakable things.

"I wanted him to kill you," his mother continued, in that terrible croaking whisper. "It was his idea so I told him he should be the one to do it. He has much more experience with these things. But he wouldn't." Her laughter sounded like fabric tearing. "He couldn't kill a child, he said. Anything else, but not a child. How noble of him to leave me with the dirty work. I have to admit though…I kinda liked it."

"Please stop." The poker felt like a sword in Peregrine's hand, a blade he could use to slice open this darkness and free himself.

"So here I am. And here you are, and one of us will die."

This was not his mother. This was some corrupt thing—the monster he'd always feared lived beneath his bed. He wanted to cry. He wanted to scream. He wanted to run. But he couldn't.

"And I won't be the one with *spine trouble*," said his mother and without warning she was sitting bolt upright, darkness flooding from her mouth, eyes filled with cold blue light. "It will be better soon, you little bastard," she said and lunged at him. But as with everything else in this skewed version of the world, her assault was slowed down by the viscous air.

Peregrine didn't move. His eyes were focused on her hands, sundering the air between them.

They were claws. No, not claws, talons, better suited to a bird of prey. And as she neared him, he saw the skin sloughing from them in messy lumps that slopped to the floor in slow motion. Her hands, he thought with a curious calm. They were the talons from the falcon on his birthday cake.

Sickened, he did the only thing he could think of.

He clutched the poker with both hands, brought it back as if preparing to hit a home run, and swung it out in front of him. And as the iron cut through the gelatinous air, everything changed.

There was no darkness.

There was no diseased woman with falcon claws.

There was no slow motion.

Only his mother, looking at him with bloodshot, barely awake eyes. "Peregrine?"

He screamed, but it was too late to slow the impetus of his weapon.

His mother opened her mouth as if to cry out and the poker hit the side of her head with a dull crunch. With a grunt, she spun sideways in a whirl of blood and auburn hair and hit the wall beside her bed face-first, hard enough to dent the plaster. Her head lolled, and for a moment she remained upright, her limbs jerking crazily. Then she fell backward, feet kicking beneath the covers as confused signals shot through her brain.

Peregrine wept and started to drop the poker. A hand on his shoulder stopped him. "You must finish it," his father said.

The boy did not look at his father, could not look away from his shuddering mother. She convulsed, right hand thumping against the wall. Her pupils overwhelmed her eyes.

"End it."

"I can't."

"You want her to suffer?"

His mother whimpered and arched her back, head snapping from side to side. She seemed to be squirming her way beneath the blankets, and when finally her struggling ceased, only her eyes could be seen above the sheet. Her chest rose and feel with impossible speed.

"I want to go."

"She's still breathing," said his father.

Sobbing, Peregrine looked at the bed. His father was right. She was not yet dead.

"Make it stop," he pleaded.

"Only you can do that. And the longer you delay, the more agony she'll have to endure. She deserves every breath of pain, but if you don't wish to see it, then put her out of her misery. Bring her to us."

Do it, said the voice inside, that sneering voice he had apparently acquired on stepping foot into the horrible new world. *Do it and get it over with. Your life won't properly begin until you do.*

With a scream of utter helplessness, rage, and sorrow, he took a single step closer to the bed, brought the poker over his head in a two-handed grip, and closed his eyes.

Before the killing blow was struck, he heard his mother whisper, in a voice not her own. *"There were turtles the size of Buicks in there. Snapping, snappity-snap."*

8

HE SAT ON A FALLEN LOG next to his father, watching the house burn. Soot and ash had made a dark mask of his face. The tracks of his tears were all that allowed a glimpse of the grieving boy beneath. But something had changed, had been *forced* to change inside him. He felt it growing in his belly, a black mass sprouting tendrils like those he'd seen spilling from his father's eyes. It promised a reprieve from the hurt, an escape from the pain, if he only let it consume him.

Something inside the house crackled and fell, and a tongue of red-yellow flame exploded from the door, sending a wave of heat rolling toward them. The breeze fanned the flames, coaxing them higher, until the house was lost within a fiery cage. His father didn't move, but Peregrine narrowed his eyes and raised a hand to shield his face. As he did so, he caught sight of something tumbling and leaping across the yard toward him. It wrapped around his right ankle and fluttered like a trapped bird.

It was the newspaper he'd seen on the kitchen table this morning.

This morning. It felt like a lifetime ago.

He picked up the paper and numbly scanned the pages, not looking for anything but feeling as though he was supposed to. Most of the paper had been lost, or burned, but on the inside page of what remained, Peregrine's eyes halted on a headline:

11-YEAR-OLD BOY RESURRECTS THE DEAD,

SOLVES MURDER!

Dirty light crept across the shadowy wasteland the past few hours had made of his mind. He looked at the grainy picture of the smiling boy—

Let him run let him go let him get away—and read the story.

I've seen him.

When he was done, he looked up at the inferno, the heat now so intense his clothes were starting to scorch him, and stood.

"I want to know why I'm here, why this is happening to me," he said. For the first time his father offered a smile that even his mangled mouth couldn't spoil.

"It's happening because it's supposed to," his father replied.

Peregrine showed him the crumpled soot-stained newspaper page. With one trembling finger, he indicated the smiling child. "And I want to know who this is."

"That," his father replied, "is your brother."

<h1 style="text-align:center">BONUS SHORT STORY</h1>
"The Neighborhood Horror Story"

"I WASN'T SURE YOU'D AGREE to this," the girl said, with another flick of her long blonde hair. "Not after...you know, all those other people asking for the same thing."

"You remember that?" Timmy asked, as he got out of the truck, took her wheelchair from the back of the truck, and went around to the passenger side to help her out of the vehicle.

"Oh sure," she told him as she opened the door and turned to face him. "It was on the news, in the papers. For a while it seemed like everywhere you looked you saw your picture. You were the talk of the town."

"It's a small town," he said. "Not hard to be the talk of it."

She nodded, watched him unfold the wheelchair and set it facing her close to the running board of the truck. "There were plenty of shots of all those crowds outside your house, too. The vigils, the masses...it had to be hard."

"It was."

"I have to admit, with more than a little guilt, that I appreciated not being the neighborhood horror story for a while." She glanced down at her legs. "Sorry."

"It's okay. I don't blame you."

He sensed her staring up at him, a small smile on her lips. "You've changed a lot."

"Time'll do that." He wished she'd stop talking, stop flirting, wished she'd quit being so goddamned nice, so goddamned *normal* because, though she had no way of knowing it, this was going to be anything but normal.

She reached her arms out to him, a perfectly ordinary action intended to indicate that she was ready for him to help her into the wheelchair, and yet coupled with the glimmer in her beautiful eyes and the slight smile on her small pink lips, it looked to him like she was inviting him into her arms instead of the other way around.

Reluctantly, he leaned into her, her perfume setting his senses alight, her hair soft against his cheek and he lifted her out of the car and gently set her down into the wheelchair. It was not difficult, for she weighed next to nothing. Letting her go, however, was not quite so easy. Her cheek brushed against his, her lips close to his ear, and he was sure for a moment that he was going to kiss her.

Get a hold of yourself, for Chrissakes.

Flustered, he released her and stepped away, the momentary flicker of disappointment on her face telling him that whatever the moment had been, she had felt it too.

She sighed and looked around. "Everything's changed."

She was right. While time had chipped away at Timmy's heart and crumbled much of his spirit, the land, his one-time home, had suffered more. The developers had claimed most of it. The pond still lay forgotten beneath the large white house, which stood like a futuristic headstone atop the hard-packed dirt. More of the trees were gone, a scant few pines all that remained to sate the aesthetic demands of the new residents. Ironically, in place of the dense stand of trees Timmy recalled from his childhood, someone had planted saplings. *Out with the old...*

The weeds had embraced whatever the developers had shunned, the grass growing tall and thick along both sides of the railroad track, unfazed by the passage of the steel behemoths through their domain. Beyond it, the field in which Timmy had reunited Jack Knox with his son had been completely overrun by brambles and witchgrass, sealing its memories in forever.

"What should I say?"

He looked at the girl, so pretty in her pink sweater that it made him ache. Her hair blew in a sudden gust of wind, and she clucked her tongue. She was not vain, Timmy realized, not obsessed with her looks, merely worried about her appearance today, now, when it mattered most. His gaze fell to the wheelchair in which she sat, to the stumps of her legs clad in folded up jeans.

Behind them, the truck he had driven to get them here— his father's battered old Chevy—still idled, the exhaust giving an occasional chagrinned rattle, as if more aware than its passengers of what was coming. Timmy remembered the rose scent of the girl's perfume as he'd lifted her out of the truck and set her in her chair, the faint tremble of her arms as she clutched him tight.

He couldn't do this.

He had to do this.

But dear God he wished he didn't.

"Say whatever you think you need to," he told her. "If over the years you've rehearsed what you might have said to him given the chance, now would be the time to use it."

"I don't know what to say."

"It'll come to you."

After a few moments of silence, she looked at him. "Do you feel sorry for me?"

He avoided her eyes. "I guess."

"A lot of people do, I suppose, but they shouldn't. Sure, it's more difficult to live life this way, but I wouldn't change it for anything. Except maybe if it brought my brother back. I guess that's why I'm here."

Timmy didn't tell her that it was not her disability that filled him with sympathy for her.

She looked up and down the railroad tracks. "Do you really think he'll show? I'm sorry, I know it's a dumb question, but despite all the stories, all the talk...I just...I just wonder if it's really *real*, you know?" Her hopeful scared blue eyes peered up at him and at that moment the urge to get away from here was stronger than it had ever been before. It was not right that it had to be this way, it was not right that God had shrugged off the responsibility of deciding people's fate for them. Who the hell was he, but Timmy Quinn, just as fucked up and flawed and imperfect as everyone else? His faith was weak, his spirit weaker. Why then had he been saddled with such an awful task? It wasn't right.

He could run. It would be the easiest thing in the world to do. He had done it many times before, and in the murky miasma his life had been and would continue to be, wouldn't saving Lena Richards from her vengeful brother be a glimmer of light in the dark forever after, a hint of salvation in an otherwise hellish existence? A good memory to help counteract all the bad he'd gathered over the years?

Yes. He could run. He could get them away from here and never look back.

He'll follow you. Maybe not soon, but someday, you'll wake up to find him grinning down at you, that mutilated metal-flesh face close to yours, and maybe, just maybe, he'll have his sister's head with him.

"Timmy?"

Unlike you, Timmy 'ol boy, they have nothing but time, and there's nowhere they won't find you.

He knew it was true. Whatever rules these things might be bound by, a change was coming. The revolution would grant them the freedom they yearned for, the ability to come out from behind the Curtain. And then there would be nowhere left to hide.

"Timmy, are you okay?"

He almost looked forward to it. After all, if they could come out on their own, he wouldn't be needed anymore. But of course, once that veil fell, there would be faces in the rain he prayed nightly he'd never see again. And they would come for him.

"What's the matter?"

Then he felt it, a tightening of the air that made his ears pop, heard the distant *ting* of a bell.

He looked at the girl and tried to smile. Tried and failed. "I'm sorry," he said, and put his hand on her shoulder. "You won't believe me, but I'm so very sorry. You have to know that I don't have a choice. That's what nobody ever seems to understand, what nobody *wants* to understand." His voice cracked on the last word, and he turned away, began to walk back to the truck. Mired on the slight gravel incline to the rails, Lena tried frantically to turn her wheelchair around.

"Wait, where are you going?"

Timmy blinked away the tears and kept walking, Lena's panicked cries like arrows into his back. "Away," he whispered and tried to fill his mind with a song, any song to drown out the distant sound of engines as the earth beneath his feet began to tremble. But he couldn't, and when at last he reached the truck, he quickly keyed the engine and turned on the radio.

"Your brother says you killed him," he whispered, and tried not to watch the rearview mirror as a dark shape, more metal than flesh, twisted its way up between the rails next to Lena like a sudden expulsion of smoke from a toxic rent in the earth.

Bring her to me, Quinn. She doesn't get to breathe while I suck gravel and dirt. Bring her to me and let me show her that there are worse things than losing your legs. Did you know she pushed me under that train? Wanted so bad to win our race she cut in front of me and her back tire collided with mine. She'll say it was an accident, of course, but her pride caused my fall.

What had happened to Lena Richards and her brother Danny had always been the cautionary tale used to keep curious children from venturing too close to the railroad tracks. For a long time, it had kept Timmy and his friend Pete away. But now all the children had grown up and moved away, and the story had died.

But today, the true neighborhood horror story had taken Lena back to the site where her brother had been sucked under a train and she had lost her legs.

Surely that should have been punishment enough.

He closed his eyes, opening them only briefly when he realized the engine and the radio combined were not enough to drown out Lena's screams as her brother came for her.

It's only enough when they say it is, he realized.

Gritting his teeth against the horror and the self-hatred, he turned up the radio and let Hank Williams' soulful crooning fill the cab as he slowly put the truck in gear.

And when at last he braved another look in the mirror, there was nothing to see but the rusted railroad tracks and an empty, overturned wheelchair.

Timmy drove home, where as always, the nightmares would be waiting in the shadows.

BONUS SHORT STORY

"Genesis"

1895

MATHESON AWOKE WITH A WOMAN'S name on his lips and a bullet hole in his chest. When he rolled off the couch, the first came slithering painfully from between his clenched teeth, the second sucking the breath in through a fiery vortex somewhere east of his heart. He dropped to the floor, nausea clutching at his throat, making him gasp for air that seemed in desperately short supply. Eyes watery with tears, he was nevertheless able to make out the deep burgundy carpet spread out around his hand like blood. *The drawing room,* he realized as another breath caught somewhere it shouldn't have, making him want to retch and gasp at the same time. Pain tickled his throat and painted his tongue with the taste of copper. On all fours, he raised one quivering hand and brought it to the wound. His white shirt was sodden red, his black dinner jacket still slung over the arm of the couch where he remembered Professor Canavan had tossed it shortly after Matheson arrived. The ragged hole seeped blood, but the oozing was slow and not at all critical, it seemed, unless of course he had already died, and the behavior of mortal wounds differed in the afterlife. He was no doctor, however, so finding someone who knew more about the ramifications of such a wound seemed the most logical step. But that would require rising, and the thought of it made him sick to his stomach.

Remembering distracted him.

Canavan's face swum into his addled brain, a mirror image dusted with pain. The professor was beaming, his eyes more alive than Matheson could ever recall seeing them before. *You won't believe it, old friend,* he'd said, his excitement almost palpable. *You won't believe it when you see what I've done.* And while Matheson had had the good manners to smile and nod and allow the old man to take his coat before leading him into the entryway, he was a little disturbed by the professor's zeal. Given Canavan's field of research and expertise, this was hardly surprising. There was more than one person on the staff at Hartford University who thought that the old man's obsession had long ago sent him waltzing into the ugly dark, from which there was no hope of return. And unlike Canavan's own theories, this dark existed purely in his own mind.

But Matheson had accepted his old friend's invitation, ostensibly to hear Canavan's news, but also because he knew the professor's daughter Cynthia would be in attendance. He had been willing to endure hours of her father's pontifications if she were in the room with him, and though twelve years his junior, he had sensed on previous visits an admiration in her for the breadth of his botanical knowledge and the gentleness with which he shared it, a sharp contrast to her father's melodramatic and vociferous outbursts of fancy. Such admiration could hardly be taken as solid interest, but it was a foundation on which he hoped to build a romance. He had no doubt that her father would object, simply because it was expected of him, and because it might lose him the only member of his immediate family still too young to have flown the roost. But in time he would realize that such protestations would result in nothing but time away from the experiments and equations that had consumed him for so very long. He would return to them with a disgusted flap of his hand, and Cynthia would be his.

But this night in Canavan House had been anything but romantic, and waking up from his slumber had not convinced Matheson it had been anything less than a nightmare. The burning hole in his chest made sure of that.

He managed to rise, one bloody hand splayed on the arm of the couch for support, his head filled with tumbling rocks that set off sparks behind his eyes and threatened to pull him back to the floor. For a brief moment his thoughts swept away from him and he panicked, shook his head to clear it, and took a very tentative step forward.

Canavan went mad, he thought, and the lucidity of it reassured him. He was not going to faint, not going to give in to the seductive pull of unconsciousness. *Stark, raving mad.*

The agony increased the further he went. He squinted against it, one hand hovering over the wound, afraid to touch it. He looked up and saw the door to the hall was ajar. Little light waited beyond it.

He went mad, and he shot me. The memory gave him pause, but as soon as gravity began to coax him again, tugging on invisible threads that had spun from the bullet hole, he moved on. Gilt-framed portraits of distinguished gentleman viewed him with disinterest as he staggered forth, breathless and shaking.

It was not the memory that had halted him, but concern, for only now had it reminded him of the other guests--the curious assemblage gathered here at Canavan's request--who had greeted him in this very room.

He stopped again, frowned and glanced to his left where there stood a large oval mahogany table, draped in a skin of lace and studded with lighted candles. A gentle breeze from somewhere nudged the flames.

There were seven of them, he remembered, seven women varying in age from prepubescent to elderly, all of them gathered at that table with their curios and symbols—he spotted colored stones, parchment pages, an ankh, a crucifix, a battered old doll missing an eye, even a Ouija Board—and all of them wearing beatific smiles as if they had come prepared to raise Jesus Christ himself, and not just the common dead.

"Psychics?" Matheson had asked, careful to keep the skepticism from his tone.

Canavan had clucked his tongue in annoyance. "Not *psychics*, man. *Receivers.*"

Matheson had no idea what the difference was, and cared even less to find out, so he'd nodded politely to the women as they were introduced, then excused himself to the bathroom. When he'd returned, they were gone, only his dearest Cynthia waiting for him.

He could no longer remember their names, but the memory of the 'receivers' faces, so eager and full of excitement, now filled him with dread. He'd guessed that what Canavan was planning would be something dramatic, it was the nature of both the man and his obsession, but the sight of those women, despite his conviction that their abilities were completely fraudulent, troubled him deeply.

At last, he reached the door, though the journey had seemed as long and arduous as a trek across the Sahara. He stopped for breath, one hand already gripping the doorknob as if fearing it might disappear if he dallied too long.

The candles fluttered. A soft breeze swept across the drawing room's tall arched windows. It was night beyond the glass, but Matheson had no idea how late it might be. The house was quiet, though that was hardly comforting. He imagined the sextet of charlatans whimpering under the threat of Canavan's gun in one of the other rooms. Would Cynthia be among them? Of course she would. Despite the professor's abrupt descent into madness, he'd never have hurt his own daughter.

Unless he thought she betrayed him too.

It was an awful thought and he willed it away. It made his head ache and he winced. His chest felt as if acid had been poured into the hole and was even now finding its way through his veins.

She'll be all right. I know she will. She must.

Resolute, he composed himself as much as the injury and fear would allow, eased open the drawing room door, and stepped into the dark hallway.

* * *

The lights in the hall were out, the only illumination provided by the carriage lamps outside the front door, their feeble amber glow casting a confusion of jaundiced shadows across the walls and floor. Matheson's shoes dragged across the tile. He was fading, but hoped his sudden lethargy had come about at the thought of another long walk rather than because of blood loss, or worse.

It bothered him, now that he thought about it. There should have been more blood. Even though his shirt was soaked with the stuff, the hole itself had stopped bleeding. He wanted to believe it was because the injury was superficial, that maybe he'd survived because Canavan knew about as much about guns and ammunition as Matheson did about flesh wounds and coagulation, but it still puzzled him. He couldn't probe the wound, or test the depth of it—he'd vomit, or worse, lose consciousness if he dared—but it *felt* deep, and the pain was excruciating, almost as if his chest was caught in a slowly tightening vice while an invisible torturer thrust a red-hot poker into his breast.

He struggled on, leaning against the wall for support. Once, he tried to cry out, but stopped himself in time. He had no idea where Canavan was, no idea where *anyone* was, and alerting them to his presence might end in disaster. At least if the professor thought him dead, he had the element of surprise on his side.

Do you believe in Purgatory, Jim?

Canavan's question, posed some weeks before in the professor's office at the University, had not come as a surprise, particularly given the title of the book he'd had spread open in front of him when he'd asked it. It was a battered red leather-bound single volume of *The Apocrypha Obscura.*

"Do you believe our loved ones go on to a better place despite their sins? Or do you think the slightest of missteps is enough to guarantee them, and us, a place in Hell? And would you, if you knew how, attempt to save them, to bring them back and spare their suffering?"

"I don't know," Matheson had answered truthfully. It was a question he'd assumed hypothetical, as any rational man would, but it quickly became clear that Canavan saw it as much more than that.

"If your wife or lover leaves you and you think of precisely the right thing to say to keep them with you for another while, would you not try to reach them at the train station, on the platform, in those last few moments before they board that train and begin the journey to their final destination? Would you not try to save them if you knew nothing but pain and suffering awaited them at the other end?"

"I suppose so, yes. But I don't understand what—"

"That, my good friend, is what I hope to achieve. Salvation for the suffering, the opening of a door that will enable us to give peace to the tormented."

After that, he'd said no more, for which Matheson had been deeply grateful. The more he listened to his friend and colleague, the more he became convinced Canavan's work had consumed and affected his brain. He supposed the death of the professor's wife had been the catalyst, turning dutiful study to frantic research, and in the weeks that followed, Canavan confirmed it.

"Are you free next Friday night?"

"I'm not entirely sure. I'll have to check my engagements. Why do you ask?"

"I'm holding something of a get-together at my house. A few friends, a few toasts, to celebrate."

"To celebrate what?"

"Ah, but it wouldn't be half the fun if I told you now. Can I assume any previous engagements can be rescheduled in favor of my little soirée? I promise you won't regret it."

Though reluctant to accept an invitation from a friend who seemed to be quickly coming apart at the seams, the idea of seeing Cynthia again made the decision an easy one.

* * *

Up ahead there was a narrow band of hazy light beneath the library door. Matheson focused on it as he shuffled his way forward, almost knocking over a planter he hadn't seen in the gloom.

The pain was unbearable now, every step punctuated by a ragged hiss, a poor substitute for a scream he couldn't allow himself for fear of detection. The advantage he'd been counting on seemed ridiculous now. He was losing strength at a rapid rate. In his present condition if he 'surprised' Canavan, the professor would have ample time and opportunity to reload his gun and finish the job he'd started. But the alternative course of turning around and heading away from the house was quickly dismissed. There were still people here, and though weak, he was no coward. He could not, in good conscience, flee this place knowing others were still in danger.

Golden specks lit his vision and he paused again, his breath sounding like a pneumatic pump as it escaped him. In the instant he closed his eyes, he relived the memory of Canavan storming into the drawing room, face a portrait of rage. At Matheson's side, Cynthia stood, her own ire a softer but no less potent reflection of her father's.

"Is this what you came for?" Canavan shouted, one hand behind his back, the other clenched by his side. "My daughter? Are you so vacuous that you'd abandon the most spectacular scientific pursuits of our time to fondle my youngest child? Get out of my house."

"He's not going anywhere," Cynthia said, raising her chin in defiance and slipping her hand into Matheson's. He remembered wishing she hadn't done it, for it was clear it was an act of rebellion meant to provoke her father further, and not a gesture borne of affection. "I wish him to stay."

"What you wish doesn't matter to me." The look of contempt that crossed Canavan's face was so powerful it elicited a gasp from his daughter. "Step away from him."

Matheson had not yet begun to panic, though he could feel it gathering its troops in the hills behind his courage. "We were just talking, Canavan, nothing more. Please, you're overreacting."

"Am I?" the professor said, and brought his other hand out from behind his back. In it, he held a pistol, which he leveled at Matheson. "I've seen you watching her, seen the lechery in your eyes. You haven't an ounce of interest in my studies. None! So enshrouded have I been in them that I've failed to see your true agenda." He nodded. "But I see it now."

"Canavan, this is madness," Matheson said, his hands floating out to placate the man. "You're mistaken."

Matheson opened his eyes, sparing himself the memory of the roar, the smoke, Cynthia's scream, the feeling of being punched in the chest by a massive fist, and, just before the trigger was pulled, Canavan's gleeful reply, *As are you, my friend.*

* * *

He reached the library and collapsed against the door, entrusting his weight to the heavy polished oak. The air seemed thicker now, and darker, as if the dust had swollen. It made it hard to breathe. His nose tickled and he rubbed it until it was sore.

He shot me. A single pulse of anger flashed through him at the thought that his old friend had tried to kill him, and for nothing. He hadn't even touched Cynthia, no matter how much he'd wanted to. Sitting next to her had been enough, basking in the intoxicating smell of her, being close enough to study her soft pink lips, the slender slope of her cheek, the ginger-colored fall of her hair. The promise that maybe in the weeks to come she would accept his kiss, accept his advances without hesitation, sated him.

With considerable effort, he turned the knob on the library door. It resisted, then gave, and swung open with a groan.

Please let her be alive.

As the room came into view, he saw it shimmer and wobble, as if he were gazing into a poorly lit aquarium. He brought a hand to his eyes, shielding them from the disorientation he hoped was the fault of the room and its feeble light and not a product of his waning consciousness. But when he looked again, the air was still thick and shifting, a carnival mirror with amber glass.

And through the oddly rolling waves of dust, he saw that all of them were there. All of them, watching him with fear etched on their honey-colored faces.

The charlatans sat in a ragged semicircle around another oval table, almost an exact duplicate of the one he'd seen in the drawing room, right down to the lace cloth and drooling candles, which burned slowly with sepia fire. It might, Matheson supposed, be the expectancy thickening the air, for he could feel it radiating from the assembly. Their eyes were wide and frightened, their mouths agape, each of the 'receivers' clutching the tools of their trade tightly to quivering breasts. Cynthia sat among them, her pallid face wet with tears, washing away some of her beauty, but despite his sluggishness, Matheson felt elation coarse through him.

She's alive. Somehow, he'd known she would be; the certainty felt like the lure that had drawn him to this room.

He smiled. "He didn't hurt you."

Everyone in the room jolted upright at the sound of his voice, startling him in turn. And from the stacks of books that lined the walls, a shadow detached itself, crossed the room and stopped in front of him.

Even through the strange amber filter the air had become, Canavan looked euphoric, none of the madness Matheson had seen in his face earlier in evidence now.

"You made it," he said, studying Matheson from top to bottom. "I knew you would."

Matheson frowned and tried to take a substantial enough breath to allow him to sound threatening. He couldn't, and the effort drained him further. His legs felt numb and now he clutched the doorjamb for support. "I need help. I'm hurt," he whispered and again watched his words make ripples in the faces of the gathering. *They're looking at me as if* I'm *the madman*, he thought, his gaze coming to rest on Cynthia's horrified expression as she wept anew.

"You look wonderful, old friend," Canavan said, unable to disguise the awe in his voice.

Matheson tried to take a step forward but his foot refused to move. "Wonder...ful? I need a doctor. You shot me. I'm dying," he said, and knew all of it to be true. "*Please.*"

He suddenly, desperately, wanted nothing more than to sleep, just for a little while. Anything to make recede the raging tide of agony lapping at his insides.

Canavan shook his head and smiled. His voice sounded very far away. "My friend, you are a hero," he said. "And soon pain will not be something you'll need to worry about. You're already dead, you see, and in coming back, you've not only validated my theories and made my experiment a success, but you've also given me the opportunity to help you."

Matheson snorted laughter and it hurt his head. He closed his eyes, praying for an end to the insanity, whomever or whatever the source. "I need a doctor," he repeated. "And the police."

Cynthia sobbed aloud, momentarily drawing the attention of everyone in the room. She raised a crumpled linen handkerchief over her eyes.

Why won't she look at me? Matheson thought, alarmed. *What's going on?* Then a terrible possibility dawned on him. Was it conceivable that she he had worked in collusion with her deranged father? Had her interest been a trap, meant to lead him away from the group so he could be murdered in private? But surely Canavan would have feared being heard? After all, his chosen method of execution was hardly subtle.

Unless...

The next thought almost robbed him of consciousness then and there, so terrible were the implications of it.

Unless they're all *in on it.*

He moaned, and noticed a moment later that the blood had begun to run again. It was warm against his otherwise cold flesh, but the pain was no more, no less than it had been before.

"Splendid, isn't it?" Canavan addressed the crowd of fearful watchers like a ringmaster at a circus. "We've done it, ladies. We've discovered the Door to Purgatory!"

"You're insane," Matheson said. "This is the bloody...door to your hall. I'm not dead, despite your efforts, and when I recover, my first order of...business will be to see you hanged."

Canavan turned back to him. "What is it like?"

Matheson said nothing. It was getting harder to breathe and the sight of all their faces being pulled by the watery air made him nauseous.

"What does it feel like where you are now?" The professor didn't wait for an answer. He was alight with excitement, barely content to await the responses his professional curiosity demanded. "How do you feel?"

How do I feel?

What is wrong with the air?

What is wrong with the women?

What is wrong with me?

Too many questions. He wanted to wake up and find himself home in bed, safe and sound beneath the covers and out of this outrageous fantasy. He was not dead, of course he wasn't, but there was something afoot here, something critical he was too feeble and tired to grasp.

He opened his mouth to speak, but it was Cynthia's voice he heard.

"Make him go away, Father. I beg you, let him go."

It's all right, Matheson wanted to assure her but the words wouldn't come, so he had to hope she'd read them in his eyes, though it was getting hard to keep them from closing. *I won't leave without you. He can't make me leave you in this madhouse.*

"Father, please. Look at him! He's suffered enough."

Canavan sighed. "My dear, I thought you understood. He's here because I, *we*, summoned him here. We're not going to add to his suffering. We're going to take it away from him, so he can go on to wherever he's bound without pain."

"This is blasphemy," Cynthia said. "You're meddling with things you have no business meddling with. You cannot influence ghosts!"

I'm not a ghost. Matheson's head began to sink. *I'm alive.*

"He's not a ghost," Canavan told her, as if Matheson had transmitted the thought to him. "He's significantly more than that. We've made history tonight, ladies. We'll all forever be remembered as mortals who unlocked Purgatory. And he's going to be our subject."

Kill him.

Matheson's raised his head, his eyes drifting dreamily from one face to the next.

After a muddled moment, he found that there was someone there now he hadn't noticed before, a shadow, darker than any of the others, standing behind the ladies at the oval table. Its head was misshapen, the body too lithe to be natural.

Kill him, it said. Now that he had recognized it, Matheson was sure he'd found the source of the voice, despite it seeming to come from inside himself. *He's a murderer, a fool, and he's set us free. Now kill him.*

"How?" Matheson mumbled aloud.

Canavan, mistakenly assuming the question was directed his way, grinned. "We're going to study you, unlock the secrets of your new domain, discover how much of you is taken with you to that awful prison. You'll achieve an importance in death you could never have dared dream of in life. You, my old friend, are the key to everything."

"I'm not dead."

Yes you are.

Matheson looked at the shadow looming over the women at the table. "Who are you?"

Canavan frowned. "Oh, come now, you know who—"

I'm you, and everything you've become. Now have your revenge on this imbecilic old fool.

"I don't know how."

"Who is he talking to?" one of the women at the table said, as symbols were raised and orbs consulted. The youngest of the group, a girl with hair the air made weave around her head like snakes, said tonelessly, "There's someone else here with him."

Cynthia rose and crossed the room. "For God's sake, Father, this has gone far enough!" Matheson followed her terrified gaze to an apparatus he had failed to notice before. It stood beside the door, large as a bureau, a contraption made of dark oak, with all manner of coils and devices hissing and spitting sparks and tongues of electricity, while dials peaked and hummed beneath a protective bell-shaped glass case.

Cynthia headed for it, pretty face set in grim determination, but her father moved with a speed that belied his years. "Don't," he warned, one finger thrust in her face. "I'm telling you: don't."

"Father, get out of my way. You have to stop this."

"The most miraculous and important discovery of our time? You want to stop it?" He shook his head in amazement and turned to point at Matheson. "You want to stop a machine that can do *this?* Are you *mad?*"

"No," she said, averting her gaze. "But I fear you are." Defeated, she marched back to her seat and sat, not looking at Matheson, who felt an ache inside him for her. It was lost in the torrent of pain and he winced, felt something surge up and out of him. He sagged against the frame, then just as quickly felt his spine contort, forcing him to stand. Something cracked and new pain blossomed in his neck, twisting his head back and forth.

"What's happening to him?"

"Canavan, it may have gone far enough. I'm sensing a peculiar amount of negative energy now."

"Is he dying?"

"You...For Heaven's sake, he's *dead!* Why can't anyone understand that! I killed the bastard and yet here he stands on a threshold that no longer leads only into my darkened hallway, but into another plane, into the fields from which God and Satan pluck their fruit! Here before us is the proof man has sought for an eternity. Here, is nothing less than—"

KILL HIM.

There was a buzzing in Matheson's head. He raised his hands as if to contain it and black fire burst from his mouth, eyes, and ears. He screamed in utter terror, pain...and finally rage, as he thrashed at imaginary bonds and shoved himself away from the wall. A thousand voices filled his head, goading him, mocking him, driving him to do what it was now clear he had to do if he hoped to survive. He had to kill the source of all this wickedness and hate. He had to kill Canavan.

The old man whirled as the air around him became a vortex. Shadows crept from the doorway and clambered up the walls, stealing the light and scaling their way up and across the ceiling. The room was alive with them. The ladies began to scream. Cynthia ran, though there was nowhere to go. She hid, with the youngest of the receivers, under the oval table. Canavan barked commands, but there was fear in his voice now.

"Canavan," Matheson said as the shadows slipped inside him, changing him, painting his eyes with darkness, giving him the sight and strength he would need to escape this hellish place to which the professor had condemned him.

Canavan backed further into the room. The women's screams continued unabated, increasing in pitch as the shadows flattened themselves and began to ooze down the walls. On all four, thick glutinous streams ran down over the baseboards, and crept across the floor like tar, toward where the women were huddled and desperately trying to escape.

"This is not how it's supposed to be," Canavan said angrily. "We were so careful!"

The pain was still tearing at his insides. Matheson could feel it, but it no longer presided over him. Now rage and an overwhelming bloodlust had taken hold of him, and he welcomed the distraction.

"I followed the passages precisely, don't you understand? I brought only the best receivers in to draw you. Their energy, the spells, the machine, *The Apocrypha Obscura*...it was all perfect. I checked it myself...a thousand times before I dared open the door! This cannot be. I won't allow it!"

Cynthia screamed, and Matheson glanced at where she was lying, something resembling a tar-covered dog standing over her, its jaw lowered to her throat.

He felt nothing.

Canavan followed Matheson's gaze, and his daughter's screams, and started to go to her. Matheson's hand on his shoulder stopped him cold.

"I'm not your experiment," Matheson told him, some distant part of him jarred by the sound of his voice, for it was not one he recognized. "And you'll be the one remembered, but not for your accomplishments." His grip on the old man's shoulder tightened, almost of its own volition, and Canavan began to lean into it, a moan escaping him. Matheson clenched his teeth together so hard they cracked and began to splinter. Fury made him shudder. He watched as his other hand reached out, the fingers pale, marked only by the jet-black veins he could see beneath the skin, and reached around to grab Canavan's jaw.

The shadows crowded the room, the screaming all but finished but for the few still audible beneath undulating skins of tar, then that too came to an end.

"Please, this is not how it's supposed to be," Canavan protested, his voice strained as Matheson, one hand still holding him in place, began to slowly, carefully, turn the old man's head around to face him.

"Now," Matheson said, "it is *you* who is mistaken."

<u>**The Timmy Quinn series**</u>

Book 1: *The Turtle Boy*

Book 2: *The Hides*

Book 3: *Vessels*

Book 4: *Peregrine's Tale*

Book 5: Nemesis: *The Death of Timmy Quinn*

ABOUT THE AUTHOR

Hailed by _Booklist_ as "one of the most clever and original talents in contemporary horror," Kealan Patrick Burke was born and raised in Ireland and emigrated to the United States a few weeks before 9/11. Since then, he has written five novels, among them the popular southern gothic slasher _Kin_ and over two hundred short stories and novellas, including _Sour Candy_ and _The House on Abigail Lane_, both of which have been optioned for film.

A five-time Bram Stoker Award-nominee, Burke won the award in 2005 for his coming-of-age novella _The Turtle Boy_, the first book in the acclaimed Timmy Quinn series.

As editor, he helmed the anthologies _Night Visions 12_, _Taverns of the Dead_, and _Quietly Now_, a tribute anthology to one of Burke's influences, the late Charles L. Grant.

Most recently, he adapted his work to comic book format for four volumes of John Carpenter's _Tales for a Halloween Night_ series of anthologies and contributed a short story to Mike Mignola and Christopher Golden's _Hellboy: An Assortment of Horrors_. He is currently at work on a new novel, _Mr. Stitch_.

Kealan is represented by Merrilee Heifetz at Writers House and Kassie Evashevski at Anonymous Content.

He lives in an unhaunted house in Ohio with a Scooby Doo lookalike rescue named Red.

You can find him on the web at kealanpatrickburke.com or on Twitter @kealanburke